THE
YOWIE
IS VERY BRAVE

THE
YOWIE
IS VERY BRAVE

Written by ANN FERNS
Illustrated by TRISTAN PARRY

The river was like a wide, silver ribbon threading its way past green, shady trees.

The Yowie sat down on the bank and pulled off his slippers and mittens. Then he wriggled his hot, aching toes and looked longingly at the water.

"Yoweeee!" he cried and slid down the bank until his feet went "splash" into the river. He wriggled his toes again and they felt lovely.

"Can you swim?" asked a sharp little voice from behind him. A small, grey Joey was standing on the top of the bank.

"No," said the Yowie.

"Then you shouldn't go near the water," scolded the Joey. "You might drown."

Quickly the Yowie pulled his feet out of the water.

"I know what you are," said the Joey. "You're a camel."

"No I'm not," said the Yowie.

"Yes you are!" The Joey stamped his foot. "My mother saw a camel once. She said it was big and yellow and furry."

"**W**ell it wasn't me that she saw," said the Yowie, " because I'm a Yowie".
The Joey suddenly began to squeak, "Help! help! help!"
"What's wrong?" asked the Yowie, looking round for the danger.
The Joey squeaked even louder. "The Yowie's got me! The Yowie's got me!"
"I have *not*!" The Yowie was most upset.
The Joey stopped squeaking and said, "My mother says that Yowies are
very dangerous".
"I know," sighed the Yowie. "Everyone thinks I'm either very dangerous or
very silly."

"I don't think you're dangerous," said the Joey.

"Thank you," said the Yowie. "Do you think I'm silly?"

"I don't know," said the Joey. "Can you do this?" and he turned a big, bouncing somersault.

"No," said the Yowie sadly.

The Joey pointed to a large gum tree that stood at the water's edge. "Can you climb that tree?" he asked.

The Yowie crossed his fingers. "Yes," he said, hoping it wasn't *too* big a fib.

"Show me," said the Joey. "Go on, climb it."

"Not just now," said the Yowie. "I don't feel like it."

"I don't believe you can!" cried the Joey. "You can't do anything!"

The Yowie looked at the tree. It seemed tall enough and strong enough and there were plenty of knobbles and branches for him to hold on to.

He decided to give it a shake, just to make sure it wasn't about to fall over.

"Great galloping goannas!" yelled a voice from the treetop. "It's a flaming earthquake!"

"No it's not," cried the Joey. "It's a Yowie!"

A very cross looking Possum stuck his face down from between the leaves and glared at them.

"A whatie?" he demanded.

"A Yowie," said the Joey again. "Some people say he's dangerous and some say he's silly."

"Well *I* say he's both if he goes round shaking trees while folks are asleep in them", snapped the Possum. "Great wobbling wallabies! I could've tumbled clean out of bed!"

"I'm very sorry," said the Yowie.

The Possum could see that he meant it, so he didn't sound quite so cross when he asked, "What did you want to shake my tree for, anyhow?"

"He wants to climb it!" squeaked the Joey, before the Yowie could answer.

"No I don't," said the Yowie quickly.

The Joey was most indignant. "Ooooh!" he said. "You said you did!"

"No," explained the Yowie. "I said I *could* climb the tree. I didn't say I wanted to."

"It's the same thing," shouted the Joey. Then he started to sing. "Scaredy old Yoweee! Daren't even climb a tree!"

In a streak of grey, woolly fur the Possum came down the tree.

"Stop that, you young larrikin!" he roared in a voice so loud that the Joey fell over backwards in the middle of his song.

Then the Possum looked up at the Yowie. "Great cackling cockatoos," he said, in a much quieter voice. "I've always said that young 'un needs putting in his place. You show him, mate. Go on, up the tree you go!"

The Yowie couldn't decide which was worse, the Joey being rude or the Possum being encouraging. Either way it looked very much as though he was going to have to climb the tree.

He wasn't quite sure how to begin. The Joey had bounced back up again and was gazing at him wide-eyed. The Possum too was watching him with great interest. They obviously thought that something rather special was about to happen.

The Yowie leapt as high as he could — which wasn't very high at all — and wrapped his arms around a stout branch. At least it was a beginning. The top half of him had begun to climb, but the bottom half of him was still dangling in space. He wasn't sure what to do about that.

His huge back feet kicked and flapped and frantically pedalled the air.

"Great polka dotted pythons!" said the Possum in admiration. "It's not the way I'd climb a tree, but it's a treat to watch."

At last the Yowie's left foot found a lump and his right foot found a bump and he was able to get his breath back and think about his next move.

It took him a long time to climb the tree. His long arms kept getting tangled in the branches and there always seemed to be one foot that had nowhere to go. Once he found that his feet were further up the tree than his hands, which gave him a terrible fright. But somehow or other, one way or another, he managed to get to the top. There he found a fork in the branches that was just the right size for his bottom, so he thankfully sat down.

"Hooray! Hooray!" the Joey hopped up and down with excitement. "The Yowie's up the tree!"

"Great bristling bandicoots!" shouted the Possum. "I couldn't have done better myself!" Which wasn't quite true, but was very kindly meant.

"Now come on down!" called the Joey.

The Yowie looked down at the ground. It was a very long way away. Coming down he would have to go backwards — and backwards you can't see where you're going!

"I'll come down later," he called back. "Much later. After you've gone."

"No!" squeaked the Joey. "I want to see you come down. Come down now!"

Slowly the Yowie turned himself round and reached down with one enormous foot until he found a branch. The branch gave a groan and bent almost double.

"Not now — later," said the Yowie, quickly sitting down in the fork again.

"There's nothing to it," said the Possum helpfully. "One quick scamper and you're down."

But the Yowie knew that he wasn't a scampering kind of animal. He lolloped and stumbled and trudged and trundled, but he never, ever scampered.

He wished that they would both go away and leave him to worry in peace. But instead of that, the crowd grew bigger. A very slow and very dusty Echidna came plodding along the river bank.

"Why are you looking up at the sky?" he asked

"We're not looking at the sky, we're looking up this tree," said the Possum.

"Oh," said the Echidna and plodded on his way. Then he turned round and plodded back again.

"Why are you looking up the tree?" he asked.

"There's a Yowie up the tree!" squeaked the Joey.

The Echidna lifted his little tube of a snout upwards and gazed into the tree. "Where?" he asked. "I can't see one."

"Just there!" cried the Possum and the Joey together.

The Echidna gazed harder. "Is it above or below the big hairy thing?" he asked at last.

"Great jumping jumbucks, it *is* the big hairy thing!" yelled the Possum.

"Oh," said the Echidna. He thought for a long time and then asked, "What is the Yoohoo doing up the tree?"

"I'm not doing anything," said the Yowie, who didn't like being discussed as though he wasn't there, "and I'm a Yowie."

"We're waiting to see him come down," explained the Joey.

"When will that be?" asked the Echidna.

"Not yet!" declared the Yowie firmly. "I like it up here."

"We don't think he *can* get down," said the Possum in a whisper that even the Yowie could hear.

Just to show that he didn't care and that he was really enjoying himself, the Yowie started to sing. He'd never sung in his life before and he was surprised to hear that he did it rather well.

"Ho! the very best place for a Yowie to be,
Is up a tree! Up a tree!
Ask a Yowie does he like climbing trees,
He'll always answer, 'Yes please, yes please!'
Willow, beech or gum tree.
Just as long as I'm up some tree.
Can't resist a jacaranda
But a pine tree's even grander,
And a clamber up a palm,
Doesn't do me any harm.
Look at me! Look at me!
Up a tree! Up a tree!"

Ｈe was just about to start on verse two when the Echidna asked another question.

"Do you think the Howlie will stay up there all night?"

The Yowie had been trying not to think about that — but now he couldn't help it. He thought about how dark it would be, how lonely it would be. The river would be deep and black as it slid along beneath him; the night birds would hoot and screech an the wind would rustle and shiver in the leaves.

Somehow he just couldn't sing verse two. There was something about his song that didn't ring true. His bottom was getting stiff and he had pins and needles in both his feet and he still didn't know how he was going to get down the tree.

Suddenly a large grey shape came leaping down the river bank and a stern voice cried, "Joey! How many times have I told you not to go near the water?"

"But Mother, there's a Yowie up this tree!" said the Joey.

Mother Kangaroo stamped her foot. "And how many times have I told you not to tell stories?"

"**B**egging your pardon, madam," said the Possum in his politest voice, "but the little fellow isn't spinning a yarn. There's a Yowie up there just as sure as I'm down here".

"The biggest Yowlie you ever saw," promised the Echidna.

Mother Kangaroo peered up through the branches. Then she gave a shriek, grabbed the Joey and stuffed him head first into her pouch.

"Shoo! Shoo! Go away you horrid creature!" She flapped her paws at the Yowie.

The Joey juggled himself the right way up and shot out of the pouch like a cork from a bottle. Up, up, he went — then down, down, and plop into the river.

"Help!" screamed Mother Kangaroo. "My baby is downing!"

"Great nibbling numbats!" yelled the Possum. "What do we do?"

The Echidna rolled himself into a ball to have a long think about the problem.

From up above there was a great rustling and creaking and then a loud "crack!". Something huge and hairy came hurtling down out of the tree.

"Whoosh! Swoosh! Splash!" An enormous fountain of water soared into the air. Millions of droplets flew in every direction. Then there was a great rippling and frothing and bubbling and up out of the water came the Yowie, with the Joey clinging round his neck.

"Oh, you dear, brave creature!" cried Mother Kangaroo as the Yowie squelched ashore.

"You said you couldn't swim!" said the Joey as he was pushed, dripping, back into the pouch.

"It only came up to my middle," explained the Yowie.

"You're a hero!" said the Possum, keeping well away from the large, wet feet.

The Echidna unrolled himself. "Why didn't you tell me the Yahoo was coming down?" he grumbled. "I wanted to watch!" And he stomped off sulkily along the river bank.

Mother Kangaroo bounded off to give her Joey a dose of eucalyptus, just in case he had caught cold. The Possum climbed back up his tree to inspect the damage. He found it much roomier without the extra branch and in five minutes he was sound asleep again.

The Yowie sat down and tried to wring the water out of his fur. It had been a funny kind of an afternoon, but perhaps not so bad. At least he had learned something — Yowies don't climb trees.

J ust as he was thinking that he might be on his way again, he heard a strange sound. In fact there were lots of sounds: feet scurrying, voices squeaking and shouting — he could even hear what they were saying.

"There he is! Yoohoo! Yoweee!"

All of a sudden he was surrounded by animals of every shape size and colour. Numbats, bandicoots, koalas, wombats and wallabies; every creature of the bush was there — including of course, Mother Kangaroo and her Joey. Even the Echidna had forgotten his sulks and was telling them all that he was a very close friend of the Yoho.

E veryone was smiling at him, patting him on the back (the smaller ones patted his ankles) and asking him to tea. They all kept saying what a brave and wonderful Yowie he was to have jumped in the river.

"It only came up to my middle," said the Yowie shyly.

But nobody heard him. What did it matter anyway? Everyone liked him, everyone wanted to be his friend. Sometimes things have a way of working out very nicely.

Published in Australia in 2004 by
New Holland Publishers (Australia) Pty Ltd
Sydney • Auckland • London • Cape Town

14 Aquatic Drive Frenchs Forest NSW 2086 Australia
218 Lake Road Northcote Auckland New Zealand
86 Edgware Road London W2 2EA United Kingdom
80 McKenzie Street Cape Town 8001 South Africa

First published by Landowne Publishing Pty Ltd 1981

ISBN 1 74110 267 7

A CiP record of this title is available from the National Library of Australia

Reproduction by Sang Choy International, Singapore
Printed in Malaysia by Times Offset

2 4 6 8 10 9 7 5 3 1